The Rabbits of West Warren Hill

Fiona E. Gow-Howell

To order additional copies of this book, contact:
Xlibris
0800-056-3182
www.xlibrispublishing.co.uk
Orders@ Xlibrispublishing.co.uk

ISBN: Softcover   978-1-9845-9438-9
       EBook   978-1-9845-9439-6

Print information available on the last page

Rev. date: 04/09/2020

Acknowledgment

In loving memory of Mac Howell.
Without whom I would not have started this book.
Always in my heart, now and forever more. 🌹

The rabbits of Westhill Warren Hill

The rabbits of Westhill Warren Hill were rather tame, they would come out and eat the dandelions the local children brought for them, the hill side was rather bare.

After school and during the holidays the children James (12), Douglas (13), and Emily (9), together with their neighbours Ian (10) and Sally (15), would play and frolic with the little rabbits, even the baby rabbits were allowed up to play in the late afternoon sunshine. That was, until he came! Jason!!

For some reason the other children didn't like him and seemed to turn their on him whenever he came near. Jason (14), had recently moved into the area with his mum. Although he had just started at the local High School, he didn't actually attend very often. Preferring to hang around the town causing a nuisance and cheeking the shop keepers. His mother just let him do what he wanted. It was easier than arguing with him, he was much stronger than she was. She feared him! Wherever he went there was a problem, he was already in trouble with the police. For what the children didn't know. All they did know was that for some strange reason they didn't like him, he smelt of trouble.

The day came when they found out just why they didn't like him. After the children James, Douglas, Emily, Ian and Sally had spent a lovely late afternoon laying on the hill with the rabbits and Emily's dog Missy, who for the best in her didn't chase them but was quite happy to run around nuzzling them, rolling over and chasing the odd stick. Before flopping down on the warm earth to doze.

In the distance they heard the shout for tea and ran in the direction of a group of nearby houses. After tea Missy wouldn't settle, she seemed very alert and pacing backwards and forwards between Emily, James and the door something was wrong, very wrong and just how bad they were about find out.

James let Missy out and straightaway she ran in the direction of West Warren Hill. The site that greeted James when he arrived a few minutes later was devastating. The hill was a gaping hole blown apart by dynamite. Jason sat smiling at the top of the hill, surveying his work. The rabbits were nowhere to be seen. At least there was no sign of any dead or injured rabbits.

Missy ran around sniffing from one place to another not sure what was going on. She knew that this was where they had been earlier playing, but now it looked and smelled differently, it smelled of evil.

James dropped to his knees by one of the shattered burrow entrances, willing with all his might to find the rabbits alive safely hidden deep in the Burrow.

Deep inside the hillside, cut off from the outside by the collapsed tunnels the rabbits lay dazed. Chuckle the rabbit chief hopped around on a bloodied injured paw, checking his troop. By some miracle none of them were dead a few cuts and no doubt bruises were the damage apart from chuckle, his paw was a mess.

Chuckle had been near the outside when Jason had appeared, and for some sixth sense had known that trouble was on its way. Having rounded up all the babies and sent everyone back deep inside the burrow he had stayed near the entrance watching not really understanding what was happening when Jason started pushing what looked like sticks into the main outside entrance hole. Chuckle sniffed the sticks and didn't like the smell. He started to head down into the hillside unfortunately not fast enough. As he hopped off his foot got caught in the blast.

Picking himself up in a daze he assessed the situation, paw hurting. But on the whole nothing too much to worry about for himself he hopped off down the tunnel dragging his injured paw to see how the rest were coping.

Jason looked over at James and threw his arms wide and shouted "Boom" and rolled onto his back laughing. Missy began to growl at him baring her teeth waiting for James to calm her, as much as he would have liked to tell her to attack, maim and kill, James knew it was wrong and called her to his side. Missy did as she was told reluctantly, the others arrived.

Jason feeling outnumbered and by now a little scared by the looks on the children's faces, as James sent Sally off to fetch his dad. He tried to make a run to escape but they were all just too quick for him and Emily and Ian had great delight in sitting on him waiting for her dad.

Sally came back with Mr Howell and the other two dogs Poppy and Macee in tow. When Mr Howell looked around at the devastating site he just shook his head and sent the dogs to seek. Soon they were tails up noses on the ground sniffing and pawing at the blown apart earth. Macee who loved digging holes and was forever being told off when she did it in the garden started digging, she was happy not to be told off this time but actually encouraged to carry on. The hole was getting larger and deeper as the dogs excavated the hillside.

Deep inside the burrow Chuckle was beginning to feel the effects of his paw injury, he lay down surrounded by his concerned children. The other bucks were investigating the collapsed tunnels looking for a way out, frightened of another tunnel collapse not really knowing the cause of the original one.

Macee stopped ears pricked listening, then sniffing the earth where she was digging and carrying on for bit then stopping to listen again. She barked a low deep bark and stood back as a hole began to open in the earth where she had just stopped digging and a small fluffy head pushed its way out through the earth thankful to see the sky again. All this while Ian and Emily were still sitting on Jason despite his cries and wails. Mr Howell called the dogs to heel and they happily trotted over to him.

Once they were clear of the entrance hole one by one the rabbits came out Chuckle was half dragged half pushed up to the entrance hole. Once at the burrow entrance he found enough strength to hop out on one back paw dragging the other behind him, he was alive!

Mr Howell walked over and lifted the injured rabbit. Chuckle, sensing that this grown human meant him no harm snuggled into his chest as he was carried back to the house. Jason was dragged to his feet and marched off in the direction of the departing Mr Howell. He had no idea what was to become of him! But he did know one thing, it was not going to be good. His dad would kill him if he were ever to find out, although from prison that would not happen soon, his mother he could deal with.

Once Mr Howell, and the children had arrived back at the house, James went with his dad to the vets Chuckles cuddling up to him on the ride, it seemed strange that this was a wild rabbit, yet snuggled like this so calm being held he felt could this be the pet that James always wanted! Yes, he had the dogs but they belong to everyone may be a rabbit could be just his. Later he would have to talk to his dad about getting a pet rabbit, but for now he was just worried about Chuckle.

All too soon they arrived at the vets carrying the rabbit in they were met by the receptionist who, looking the rabbit over in James's arms said she would get the vet so that the poor creature could be put out of his misery. James let out an ear-piercing wail and poor Chuckle leapt from his arms to be caught very skilfully by the young vet, who had just walked through the door, just at that right moment.

Seeing James's distress at what would have been the usual steps for a wild rabbit, the vet looked to Mr Howell for an explanation. Mr Howell explained that although wild the local children all played with the rabbits on the hill like pets, all but Jason!

"Well" said the vet "in that case we'll have to take a look and see if we can do anything with his paw".

So, the vet lead them into the consulting room and agreed with Mr Howell that he would do what he could but there were no guarantees that the rabbit could be saved. Mr Howell looked at James his son and said that he would foot the bill for the treatment no problems. His choice of words were, if thought about rather comical considering poor Chuckle's injury. So, armed with a bowl of warm water the young vet applied a small amount of local anaesthetic to the foot and set about cleaning the dirt and blood away from the paw.. Once that has been done, the damage was visible fortunately for Chuckle it wasn't that bad, the foot itself was mainly whole. The damage was mostly superficial the pad underneath had a large cut. The vet cleaned the cut and carefully dried it, all this time Chuckle laid quietly on the vet's table, knowing he was being helped. He seemed to realise that these humans meant him no harm. The same can't be said of Jason. With a few drops of superglue it would heal. Two of his toes and claws were hanging off these were removed, dissolvable stitches were put in and again a little bit of superglue (when I say superglue, it's like it, but for human and animal skin, works great used to seal the wound). As Chuckle was a wild rabbit there were no point in putting dressings and bandages on, as these couldn't be looked after. So, a bit more superglue and a dissolvable sock dressing was put on and he received an injection of antibiotics just in case, all was good to go.

The vet handed Chuckle to James and turned to Mr Howell and said, "not to worry about the bill it was his pleasure". Both James and Mr Howell thanked him as they left. Chuckle snuggled into his chest feeling safe. The vet had been kind to him, and he was most grateful. Falling asleep on James's knee on the way home he had no idea what was going on back at the burrow, were the others safe!

When they got back home it was late, too late for Chuckle to go back to the burrow tonight. Mrs Howell fetched an empty cardboard box laid a soft towel inside and James place Chuckle down inside on the kitchen floor for the night. Missy, Poppy and Macee having been out for their night walk laid down on the floor next to the box keeping guard. Jason wouldn't get past them to hurt Chuckle tonight they were on duty.

Back at the burrow everyone was missing Chuckle, they hoped he was okay, would he be able come back to them? They could only hope!. Surprisingly the bucks in this colony had no eagerness to lead, or take over charge, they reserved that right to Chuckle. When he died then changes would have to be made, but until then they stayed as they were.

This being said, it didn't stop them dividing the colony up into groups, and each buck taking a job as they set about renewing the tunnels structure. Piece by piece the tunnels were re-dug, the babies put back in the nursery as night fell. What a day!!

Most of the adult rabbits slept very fitfully not sure if they were really safe. They had all seen Jason being taken away but could he return! Without Chuckle a sense of unrest was settling over the colony.

The next day being Saturday meant that the children were free to visit the hill, and today was no exception. They came bringing gifts carrots, celery, and lush green grass picked from the side of the compost heap in Mr Howell's garden. They also brought with them small spades and trowels and a rake. As the rabbits had rebuilt the inside of the Warren the children were going to rebuild the outside.

James brought with him an extra special present for the colony, Chuckle was snuggled inside his jacket.

The outside ground of the hill started to take shape, the children heaped mounds of earth back into place where it had been blown away, patting it down firmly. They each made sure that holes were made in the new hill that corresponded with the existing openings of the Warren.

James laid Chuckle down gently and he hopped carefully towards the burrow.

All was at peace.

Mr Howell visited the police station to give evidence against the actions of Jason. Who had since been released into his mother's custody, with a warning to stay away from the hill.

His mother had no control over her son. To her he was a source of embarrassment, his father had ruled with a stick when he wasn't in prison for armed robbery.

Jason wouldn't say where the dynamite had come from, just how much fun he'd had using it! For now all anybody could hope for was that he stayed away from the hill.

Chuckle settled back into the Warren wary of the slightest noise. The other bucks posted sentries in the Warren tunnels. Hoping they would not hear the noise of the beast again.

Epilogue

6 months later Jason appeared before the Juvenile Court charged with vandalism, animal cruelty, animal endangerment. He pleaded guilty. Not that he had much choice, his mother saw to that. He got a job after school to pay the vets bills and compensation to Chuckle.

The Judge horrified with what he had done, but also where he got the dynamite from sentenced him to 2 years community service, working at the local animal shelter three times a week. It looks likes Jason's free time was going to be a thing of the past. What with working to pay the compensation and vets bills, and then the animal shelter.

Things on the hill went back to normal, winter came and with it the snow. The children walked the dogs at West Warren Hill taking with them apples, broccoli stalks, vegetable peelings and a carrot or two to help the burrow over the winter months.

Chuckle came out pushing snow from the burrow entrance to the sound of the children and the dogs, Macee ran over and gave him one big lick in greeting. Chuckle's paw now already healed caused no real problems. The other bucks taking on the job of any digging, as Chuckle's rear paw having lost a couple of toes, was not really up for the digging process.

The young babies of the summer we're now grown into young adults, life went on with children, dogs and rabbits enjoying each other's company.

Jason stayed away. His dad found out about the trouble, but from prison there wasn't much he could do. What bothered his dad most was that Jason had found his stash of safe blowing dynamite. Trouble was brewing, in that household!

The end